STAR WARS®

I AM A PRINCESS

By Courtney B. Carbone
Illustrated by Heather Martinez

 A GOLDEN BOOK • NEW YORK

randomhousekids.com
ISBN 978-0-7364-3605-2 (trade) — ISBN 978-0-7364-3606-9 (ebook)

Printed in the United States of America

10 9 8 7 6 5 4 3 2 1

I am a princess.
I lead others and keep them safe.

A princess is the daughter of a royal family. Princess Leia's mother was a wise and brave queen named **Padmé Amidala**. Her father, **Anakin Skywalker**, was a powerful Jedi knight—a guardian of peace.

But Leia only ever knew her adoptive parents, Senator **Bail Organa** and his wife, **Breha**.

Like her parents, Leia has an **adventurous spirit** and a strong desire for justice.

A princess will do anything to **protect** her people. When the galaxy was in the grips of the evil Empire, Princess Leia joined the rebellion to fight for what's right.

Leia delivered the Death Star plans to the rebels—and **helped** destroy the Empire's gigantic battle station!

A princess must **stand up** to her enemies . . .

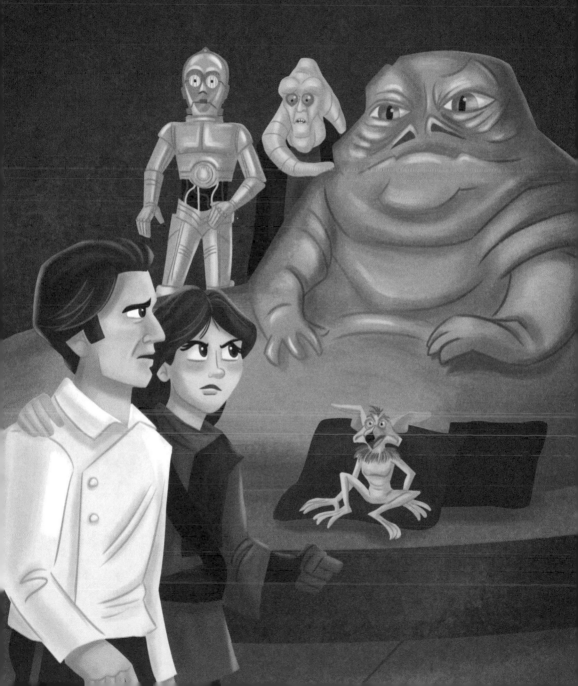

no matter how **BIG** and **MEAN** they are!

A princess must be ready to **take charge** in any situation . . .

. . . and **race** into action!

A princess is an ambassador of **peace** and goodwill. She makes new friends—and allies—wherever she goes!

Sometimes a princess may find herself in a **scary** place . . .

. . . or a **tight spot**. A princess must always be brave.

Sometimes a princess needs to be
SNEAKY to outsmart her foes. When
rebel hero **Han Solo** was captured
and frozen in carbonite, Leia disguised
herself as a bounty hunter to rescue him.

From the moment she is born, a princess **devotes** herself to the well-being of others.

A princess must **always** be a hero.

Are you ready to be a **hero**?